This book is for . . .

_____

_____

_____

_____

_____

_____

Thank you RW & VWA—RCP

If You Believe in Me
Copyright © 2022 Rosemary Wells

Published in 2022 by Red Comet Press, LLC

Library of Congress Control Number: 2021948299
ISBN (HB): 978-1-63655-016-9
ISBN (EBOOK): 978-1-63655-017-6

22 23 24 25 TLF 10 9 8 7 6 5 4 3 2 1

First Edition
Manufactured in China

RED
COMET
PRESS

RedCometPress.com

ROSEMARY WELLS

If You Believe In Me

RED COMET PRESS · BROOKLYN

I am just a little bear
Sitting in a great big tree,
Dreaming of Somehow-Someday Things
That might just happen to me.

I can turn a cartwheel.

I can dive in the waves in the sea.

And fly my kite up into the clouds because
You believe in me.

Watch me build a castle
And count to one hundred
and three.

I know my books by heart because
You believe in me.

Dark nights never scare me.
There's always a star to see.

I'm not afraid because I know
You believe in me.

When I'm alone and feeling small,
And the whole wide world is ten feet tall,

Everything changes suddenly

When you say . . .
You believe in me.

What will come tomorrow?
A rough-and-tumble day?

A storm that roars
From the end of the world?
I know I'll find my way.

The rain will wander eastward soon.
Behind it is the waiting moon.

My dreams and hopes will hold me.
I'll make them all come true.
No dream's too big
   because you told me

I believe in *you*.